MW01180770

UCLA BASKETBALL

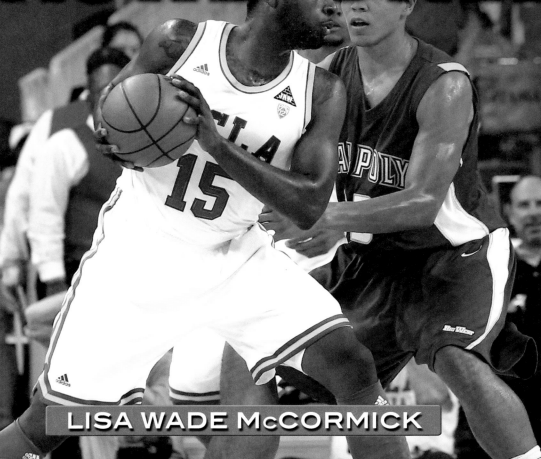

LISA WADE McCORMICK

rosen publishing's
rosen
central®
New York

Published in 2014 by The Rosen Publishing Group, Inc.
29 East 21st Street, New York, NY 10010

Library of Congress Cataloging-in-Publication Data

McCormick, Lisa Wade, 1961-
UCLA basketball/Lisa Wade McCormick.—1st ed.—New York: Rosen, c2014
    p. cm.—(America's most winning teams)
Includes bibliographical references and index.
ISBN: 978-1-4488-9408-6 (Library Binding)
ISBN: 978-1-4488-9443-7 (Paperback)
ISBN: 978-1-4488-9446-8 (6-pack)
1. University of California, Los Angeles—Basketball--History—Juvenile literature.
2. UCLA Bruins (Basketball team)—History—Juvenile literature. I. Title.
GV885.43.U423 .M33 2014
796.323'630979494

Manufactured in the United States of America

CPSIA Compliance Information: Batch #S13YA: For further information, contact Rosen Publishing, New York, New York, at 1-800-237-9932.

CONTENTS

W.B./Sebco 2016

INTRODUCTION

It's a powerhouse in college basketball—a team with some of the greatest players, coaches, and games in sports history. Which college program holds the bragging rights to these and other top honors on the hardwood? The University of California, Los Angeles (UCLA) Bruins are considered the kings of the court among the 337 Division 1 men's basketball programs in the country. This basketball dynasty started its reign in 1919 and has remained one of the most winning teams in college basketball.

UCLA entered the 2012–2013 season with an all-time record of 1,720–767. Only two college basketball teams had better records: the Kentucky Wildcats (2,089–649) and the Kansas Jayhawks (2,070–805).

The Bruins have won more national championships than any other men's basketball team in college history—a record eleven titles. The Bruins captured seven of those national crowns in back-to-back years from 1967–1973. UCLA's highlight reel is filled with other memorable moments, including:

- Its eighty-eight-game winning streak, the longest in college basketball history
- Four undefeated seasons
- Fifty-four back-to-back winning seasons (1949–2002)
- Eighteen Final Four appearances
- Thirty-two Final Four games
- Thirty regular-season conference championships

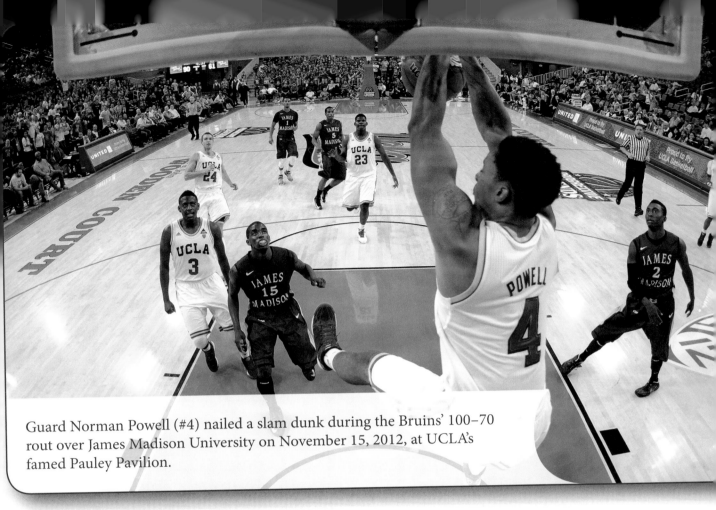

Guard Norman Powell (#4) nailed a slam dunk during the Bruins' 100–70 rout over James Madison University on November 15, 2012, at UCLA's famed Pauley Pavilion.

In addition, the Bruins played in the first nationally televised regular-season college basketball game. The Bruins lost to the Houston Cougars 71–69 in that 1968 "Game of the Century," which forever changed the landscape of college basketball.

Throughout ninety-plus seasons, UCLA has been home to some of basketball's best players and coaches. Many became Olympic champions, NBA stars, and Hall of Famers. These game changers include Lew Alcindor (who later changed his name to Kareem Abdul-Jabbar); Bill Walton; Rafer Johnson; Ed and Charles O'Bannon; and the man that ESPN called "one of the most revered coaches ever," the legendary John Wooden.

The following pages highlight some of the key players, coaches, and buzzer-beater moments that have made UCLA one of the most successful basketball teams in college history.

CHAPTER 1

THE BRUINS' EARLY YEARS

A basketball dynasty started the moment UCLA's first team stepped on the hardwood. It happened on October 3, 1919. The historic game pitted UCLA against Manual Arts High School in Los Angeles, California. UCLA—known at that time as the Southern Branch of the University of California—played high schools and other teams its first season. It wasn't part of an official college conference.

UCLA defeated Manual Arts 46–38 in its debut game. Head coach Fred W. Cozens led the team to eleven more wins during its inaugural season. Cozens was the school's athletic director, too. Team captain Si Gibbs helped UCLA finish 12–2 its first season. The team's only losses came against Redlands (21–34) and Throop (30–41).

UCLA joined the Southern California Intercollegiate Athletic Conference (SCIAC) its second season. And its reign on the hardwood continued.

Cozens and his players ended the 1920–1921 season with an 8–2 record. They also won their first conference championship. Captain Raymond McBurney and his teammates had a rocky start that season. They lost their opening game 28–36 to California.

UCLA BASKETBALL PLAYER WINS NOBEL PEACE PRIZE

The first African American to win a Nobel Peace Prize played basketball for UCLA during the 1920s. Ralph Bunche was a guard for the Bruins. During his time on the court, UCLA won three Southern Conference Championships. Bunche played for head coach Pierce "Caddy" Works. This three-sport athlete excelled at baseball and football, too. Bunche graduated in 1927 with a degree in political science. He was valedictorian of his class.

Bunche later earned a Ph.D. in government and international relations at Harvard. He was the first African American to receive a doctoral degree in that field from the Ivy League school. Bunche spent much of his career working for peace in the Middle East. He helped write the final agreement that stopped the fighting between Israel and its neighboring Arab states in 1948–1949. Bunche received the Nobel Peace Prize in 1950 for his efforts to stop the bloodshed between those warring nations.

Former UCLA guard Ralph Bunche became the first African American to win a Nobel Peace Prize. Bunche received the prestigious honor in 1950 for negotiating the 1948 Arab-Israeli treaty.

But the team quickly rebounded. UCLA won its next nine games. It fell again to California 29–46 in the season's final game. Cozens stepped down as UCLA's head coach after his second season.

WORKS LEADS UCLA FOR EIGHTEEN SEASONS

UCLA's next head coach led the team for eighteen years. Pierce "Caddy" Works served as the team's head coach from 1921 to 1939. During that time, Works and his players tallied a 173–159 record. They won six SCIAC championships. Works had winning records nine of his first ten seasons. He also coached some of UCLA's early top players, including its first all-American. Dick Linthicum earned that honor.

During Works's first season on the bench, UCLA posted a 9–1 record. That's an impressive .900 winning percentage—the highest in his career. The only loss UCLA and returning team captain Si Gibbs suffered in that 1921–1922 season came in game two. The team dropped 24–26 to Redland in a nail-biter. Two games later, UCLA held its opponent to less than ten points. It defeated Whittier 29–9.

In his fifth year on the bench, Works led UCLA to a perfect 10–0 record in conference play. Horace Bresee was the captain of that 1925–1926 team. The Bruins ended the season 14–2 overall.

UCLA joined the Pacific Coast Conference (PCC) during the 1927–1928 season. Early in the year, UCLA crushed Pomona in a nonconference 70–10 blowout. The team also won its first PCC game—a seven-point (29–22) victory over Stanford. It finished the year 5–4 in the PCC and 10–5 overall.

FIRST ALL-CONFERENCE HONORS

The Bruins reached two milestones that season, too. Forward Jack Ketchum became UCLA's first basketball player to earn all-Conference honors. The university also changed its team name from the Southern Branch to the Bruins in 1928. A bruin is a bear, according to Merriam-Webster's dictionary. Bears have served as UCLA mascots since the university was founded in 1919.

The Bruins suffered their first losing record in the school's history during the 1928–1929 season. UCLA finished 7–9 overall and 1–8 in the PCC. The team looked promising early in the season. Headed by captain Sam Balter, the Bruins won their first five games. But they later lost PCC matchups against California, Stanford, and the University of Southern California (USC).

UCLA bounced back in the 1929–1930 season. The Bruins tallied a 14–8 winning record. But they were slow off the dribble in conference play. UCLA and team captain Larry Wildes ended the season 3–6 in the PCC.

UCLA's record dropped to 9–6 during the 1930–1931 season. The Bruins won their first three games. They also crushed Montana 59–27 in the fifth game of the season. But UCLA and team captain Carl Knowles dropped close games to California (24–26) and Stanford (28–29) and ended the season 4–5 in the PCC.

THE FIRST ALL-AMERICAN

UCLA's forward Dick Linthicum etched his name in college basketball history in 1931. He became the school's first all-American that year. The award honors the best players in the country.

Linthicum earned all-American honors again the following year. He also served as UCLA's team captain. But the Bruins suffered a disappointing year. The team's record fell to 9–10 overall and 4–7 in the PCC.

UCLA continued to struggle for several years. Works and his teams didn't finish above .500 for the next seven seasons. The team posted its worst record under Works during the 1937–1938 season. UCLA finished 4–20. That's a winning percentage of just .167.

Seven UCLA players still earned all-Conference honors during those tough seasons in the 1930s. Those players were forward Carl Knowles (1930); center Frank Lubin (1931); forward Don Piper (1934); and guard Don Ashen (1935). Two UCLA players made the all-Conference team in back-to-back years: forward Dick Linthicum in 1931 and 1932, and center John Ball in 1936 and 1937. Forward Bob Calkins also won all-Conference honors in 1939.

JOHNS TAKES OVER AS HEAD COACH

UCLA tried to turn its basketball program around at the start of the 1939–1940 season. The university named former Bruins basketball player Wilbur Johns as its third head coach. Johns led the Bruins for nine seasons. He coached 213 games and ended his career on the bench with a 93–120 record. He won one regular season conference championship, and two of his players became all-Americans.

Johns's team posted its first winning record during the 1942–43 season. The Bruins finished 14–7 overall and 4–4

UCLA BASKETBALL STAR BECOMES BASEBALL LEGEND

Jackie Robinson made history in 1947 when he became the first African American to play major league baseball. But Robinson also made history as a young basketball player at UCLA. He was a forward for the Bruins from 1939 to 1941. Wilbur Johns was his coach. Robinson led the PCC in scoring both seasons. He was named the PCC's Most Valuable Player. He also earned all-Conference honors in 1940.

Robinson excelled at other college sports. He was the first Bruin to letter in four sports in one year: basketball, baseball, football, and track. Robinson was the national champion in long jump. He was an all-American halfback in football. And he played shortstop for UCLA's varsity baseball team.

Baseball legend Jackie Robinson was a star forward on UCLA's basketball team from 1939 to 1941. He was the first Bruin to letter in four sports in one year: football, baseball, basketball, and track.

in the PCC. The spunky Bruins kept fighting. And they kept getting better.

During the 1946–1947 season, UCLA won more games than any other team in the school's twenty-seven-year history. The Bruins ended the year 18–7 overall and 9–3 in the conference. Another UCLA player also stamped his name in the record books.

BARKSDALE AND PUTNAM NAMED ALL-AMERICANS

Center Don Barksdale, who averaged 14.7 points per game, became an all-American in 1947. He was the second African American in the country to receive the prestigious award. The first was George Gregory, a 6-foot-4 (193 centimeter) center for Columbia University in New York City. He was named an all-American in 1931.

Nine other UCLA players won regional and national honors during Johns's career as head coach. UCLA guard Bill Putnam was named an all-American in 1945. Guard Dave Minor made all-Conference teams in 1947 and 1948. And his teammate and fellow guard John Stanich became an all-Conference player in 1948.

Johns resigned as UCLA's head coach at the end of the 1948 season. His team had a disappointing 12–13 record and went 3–9 in the PCC during his final year on the bench. Johns didn't leave UCLA, though. He became the university's athletic director. One of his first decisions in that new role changed the course of UCLA basketball forever. Johns hired the coach who made UCLA the most winning team in the history of college basketball.

CHAPTER 2

THE WOODEN LEGACY

Sportswriters billed the game as a "showdown" between the top two basketball teams in the country. More than thirteen thousand fans packed Memorial Coliseum in Portland, Oregon, to watch the March 20, 1965, NCAA championship. UCLA—the reigning NCAA champion—faced top-ranked Michigan for college basketball's title crown.

The Bruins upset Michigan 91–80 in a matchup that coach John Wooden called the "most spectacular showing" he'd seen on the hardwood during his twenty-seven seasons at UCLA. What made this game so special to Wooden, who led UCLA to ten NCAA championships?

"I think it was Gail Goodrich's scoring 42 points against a powerful Michigan team when he was the smallest player on the court," Wooden said, according to *The Bruin 100: The Greatest Games in the History of UCLA Basketball.* That's high praise from the man who coached some of the best players and games in college history.

During his nearly three decades with the Bruins, Wooden captured more NCAA championships than any college coach on record. He won more games than any basketball coach in UCLA history. And he never had a losing season with the Bruins.

Sportscaster Al Michaels spoke during a memorial for UCLA's legendary basketball coach John Wooden. Wooden, the most winning basketball coach in Bruin history, died June 4, 2010. He was ninety-nine.

Wooden led UCLA's men's basketball team from 1948 to 1975. That's nearly one-third of the school's basketball history. He finished his career with an impressive 620–147 record. Wooden's legacy includes seven back-to-back NCAA championships (1967–1973), an eighty-eight-game winning streak (1971–1974), and four 30–0 seasons (1963–1964, 1966–1967, 1971–1972, and 1972–1973). He also coached Lew Alcindor (Kareem Abdul-Jabbar), Bill Walton, and some of the other top players in the game's history.

UCLA's Mascots

Bears have always played key roles as UCLA's mascots and team names. The school's first football team was called the Cubs. Coach Jimmie Cline switched that nickname to the Grizzlies in 1923. Five years later, UCLA changed its nickname to the Bruins.

Real or costumed bears have served as UCLA mascots since the 1930s. The school's first mascot was a live bear that attended all home football games. The school later banned the bear's appearance for safety reasons.

Little Joe Bruin, a Himalayan bear cub, became the school's mascot in the early 1950s. He became too big, and the school gave him to the circus. In 1961, UCLA picked its first female bear as the school's mascot. Josephine also became too big, and UCLA donated her to the San Diego Zoo.

Male students started to dress in bear costumes in the mid-1960s. The first female bear mascot appeared in 1967. Joe and Josephine Bruin still appear at UCLA sporting events.

UCLA mascot Joe Bruin entertains fans during the 2006 Final Four game against the Florida Gators. Joe Bruin and female mascot Josephine Bruin regularly appear at UCLA sporting events.

SNOWSTORM LEADS WOODEN TO UCLA

UCLA's basketball history might not have included those golden Wooden years if a snowstorm hadn't crippled the Midwest in the spring of 1948. The former all-American at Purdue University was the Bruins' top pick for head coach. But Wooden had his sights set on coaching at the University of Minnesota.

Minnesota officials promised to call Wooden at 6:00 PM on Saturday, April 17, 1948, if he landed the job. The call never came. An hour later, UCLA offered Wooden the position as its head coach. He accepted and agreed to leave his job as head coach at Indiana State. Later that night, Wooden heard from Minnesota. The school said no one could call earlier because a winter storm knocked out phone service in Minneapolis/St. Paul.

WINNING TRADITION STARTS

Wooden inherited a "so-so UCLA squad" when he arrived on campus, according to a December 3, 1948, story in the *Long Beach Press-Telegram.* The Bruins had lost all five starters from the previous year. Wooden built his first UCLA team around junior guard and Olympic high jumper George Stanich. The game plan worked. The thirty-eight-year-old "Rookie of Westwood" won his first game as UCLA's head coach. The Bruins defeated Santa Barbara 43–37 using Wooden's "racehorse" style of basketball.

The Bruins used that quick style of play throughout the season—and the rest of Wooden's career. UCLA went 22–7 during Wooden's first season. But the Bruins—and their tradition of winning—were just getting warmed up.

UCLA won at least fourteen games a season during Wooden's first fifteen years on the bench. The team never finished with a record under .538. And eight players became all-Americans during those early seasons.

NAULLS SETS SCHOOL RECORD

UCLA reached other milestones, too. The 1955–1956 squad posted the Bruins' first 16–0 season in the PCC. All-American Willie Naulls set a school record for rebounds during a 99–79 blowout over Arizona State. The 6-foot-5 (196 cm) center snagged twenty-eight rebounds in that January 28, 1956, contest.

Two years later, Olympic track-and-field star Rafer Johnson became a key playmaker for the Bruins. He scored 16 points in his first game as a starter. UCLA finished its 1958–1959 season 16–9.

UCLA marked its worst season under Wooden the following year. The Bruins finished 14–12 in the 1959–1960 season. They quickly rebounded. For the first time in school history, the Bruins advanced to the NCAA Final Four in 1962. UCLA lost 72–20 in the semifinals to Cincinnati, the defending national champions.

UCLA WINS ITS FIRST NCAA CHAMPIONSHIP

The Bruins won their first NCAA championship in 1964. The team also posted its first 30–0 season. None of the players in UCLA's starting lineup that season were taller than 6-foot-5 (196 cm). UCLA relied on the strength and speed of guards

Coach John Wooden and his team celebrated after winning their first NCAA championship in 1964. The Bruins crushed Duke 98–83 in that title game. Wooden won ten championships at UCLA.

Gail Goodrich and Walt Hazzard, and guard/forward Kenny Washington. It also taunted teams with its tough full-court press, known as the "Bruin Blitz."

UCLA entered the 1964 championship game as underdogs against the Duke Blue Devils. "Duke had size, strength, shooting ability, and defense," Scott Howard-Cooper wrote in *The Bruin 100*. But the Bruins had their famous "Blitz." And they used it to spark a 16–0 run and trounce the Blue Devils 98–83. Goodrich led the team in scoring with 27 points.

TOURNAMENT DOMINATION

UCLA captured its second straight NCAA title in 1965. It defeated top-ranked Michigan 91–80. The team won its third NCAA championship in 1967. The victory marked the first of seven title crowns in back-to-back years.

The legendary Lew Alcindor (Kareem Abdul-Jabbar) made his debut in the Bruins lineup during the 1966–67 season. The unstoppable center scored a record 56 points in his first varsity game, a 105–90 victory over rival USC.

Former UCLA star Lew Alcindor (Kareem Abdul-Jabbar) showed off his famous sky hook during a 1968 game against Houston.

"Alcindor had proved, from the start, he would stand alone as the superior talent in college basketball," Howard-Cooper wrote in *The Bruin 100*. Alcindor led the Bruins to their second 30–0 season. The sophomore center helped UCLA win the 1967 championship, too. He grabbed 18 rebounds and scored 20 points in UCLA's 79–64 win over Dayton.

Alcindor guided the Bruins to two more NCAA championships. He scored 34 points and pulled down 16 rebounds in UCLA's crushing 78–55 defeat over North Carolina in the 1968 title game. A year later, Alcindor scored 37 points and snagged 20 rebounds in the Bruins 92–72 rout over Purdue for the 1969 national title. Alcindor was a three-time all-American during his college career.

THE ALCINDOR RULE

UCLA center Lew Alcindor became an unbeatable force on the hardwood during his college days. The 7-foot-2-inch (218 cm) center averaged 26.4 points a game with the Bruins. Alcindor had a secret weapon. He could dunk better than anyone in the game.

The NCAA worried that no one could stop Alcindor because of his dunking skills. Those concerns led the NCAA to ban dunking in college games in 1967. The action became known as the Alcindor Rule.

The decision didn't stop Alcindor from scoring. He mastered another shot—his trademark sky hook. Defenders couldn't block the high arcing shot. Alcindor used the sky hook to help the Bruins win three back-to-back NCAA championships.

The all-American took his signature move to the NBA. Alcindor, who changed his name in 1971 to Kareem Abdul-Jabbar for religious reasons, played for the Milwaukee Bucks and Los Angeles Lakers. He became the league's all-time leading scorer with 38,387 points. The NCAA lifted its ban on dunking in 1976.

UCLA'S CHAMPIONSHIP STREAK CONTINUES

UCLA's reign on the hardwood continued, even without Alcindor in the lineup. The Bruins won the NCAA championship the next four years.

Junior forward Sidney Wicks helped the Bruins defeat Jacksonville 80–69 in the 1970 championship game. Center Steve Patterson scored 29 points during UCLA's 68–62 victory over Villanova in the 1971 title game.

UCLA ended its 1970–1971 season 29–1. Its only loss came in January 1971 when the team fell to Notre Dame 82–89. The Bruins wouldn't lose another game for the next three years—or another eighty-eight games.

All-American center Bill Walton played a pivotal role in UCLA's 1972 championship title. He scored 24 points and grabbed 20 rebounds in the Bruins' 81–76 win over Florida State. UCLA ended the season with its third 30–0 record.

Walton scored 44 points in the 1973 title game and led the Bruins to another national championship. UCLA destroyed Memphis State 87–66 to capture its seventh back-to-back championship crown. The team also posted its fourth 30–0 season.

EIGHTY-EIGHT-GAME WINNING STREAK ENDS

What about UCLA's eighty-eight-game winning streak? It ended on January 19, 1974. UCLA blew an early 17-point lead and lost in the final seconds to Notre Dame 71–70. The longest winning streak in college basketball came to end when Notre

Dame's Dwight Clay nailed a 25-foot (7.62 m) jumper with twenty-nine seconds on the clock.

Another legendary winning streak in UCLA basketball's history ended a year later. The Bruins' most successful coach ever announced his retirement from the game after twenty-seven years at UCLA. Wooden's players heard the news first—in the locker room. He shared his decision to retire with the players after their narrow 75–74 win over Louisville in the 1975 NCAA semifinals.

According to *UCLA Magazine*, Wooden told his team, "I don't know how we'll do Monday night against Kentucky. But I think we'll do all right. Regardless of the outcome of the game, I never had a team give me more pleasure." He added, "I'm very proud of you. This will be the last team I'll ever coach."

Wooden ended his celebrated career at UCLA the same way he started—with a win. On March 31, 1975, UCLA defeated Kentucky 92–85 to capture its tenth NCAA crown.

"There was no way we were going to lose the coach's last game," junior guard Andre McCarter told the Associated Press after the game.

UCLA now faced a difficult decision. Who would it hire to replace Wooden? Could it find anyone to replace a coach that built what ESPN has called "one of the greatest dynasties in all of sports"?

CHAPTER 3

THE DAWN OF A NEW ERA

More than nineteen thousand people packed the St. Louis Arena on a Saturday night in November 1975. Excitement filled the air. The clash between the defending champions of UCLA and top-ranked Indiana was just moments away. The *Bloomington Daily Herald* called the game the "greatest opening a college basketball season has ever had."

But that November 29, 1975, battle between the basketball titans had a deeper, more historic meaning to Bruins fans. It marked the dawn of a new era in UCLA basketball. The game represented the first time in twenty-seven years that John Wooden wouldn't coach the Bruins. He shocked fans when he resigned earlier in the year.

UCLA hired former Illinois head coach Gene Bartow to continue Wooden's legacy on the hardwood. Bartow made his coaching debut with the Bruins in that showdown against the Hoosiers. It wasn't pretty. Indiana trampled UCLA in a 20-point blowout. The Hoosiers destroyed the Bruins 84–64 in the nationally televised game. UCLA lost its first season opener since 1964.

Gene Bartow (*right*) replaced John Wooden (*left*) as UCLA's head basketball coach in 1975. The coaches met years before Bartow took over the program. Bartow led the Bruins for two seasons.

BARTOW LEADS THE BRUINS TO FINAL FOUR

Bartow quickly turned the team around, though. The Bruins won their next fifteen games and ended the season 28–4. UCLA advanced to the NCAA tournament. The Bruins lost to Indiana 65–51 in the Final Four. The Hoosiers won the 1976 national championship.

UCLA posted another winning season the following year. All-American Marques Johnson led the Bruins to a 24–5 season. UCLA returned to the NCAA tournament but lost a 76–75 heartbreaker to Idaho State in the second round.

Bartow resigned after his second season. He compiled an overall 52–9 record with the Bruins—the second best in UCLA history.

GARY CUNNINGHAM NAMED HEAD COACH

The Bruins turned to a former UCLA star player and assistant coach to replace Bartow. Gary Cunningham, who served as Wooden's assistant for ten years, took over the reins in 1977.

Now part of the Pacific-10 Conference, the team ended its first season under Cunningham 14–0. UCLA was 25–3 overall in the 1977–1978 season. All-American forward David Greenwood helped the Bruins advance to the national tournament. UCLA lost to Arkansas 74–70 in the second round.

The Bruins fought their way to the Elite Eight the following year. UCLA fell to DePaul 95–91 in that round. The Bruins finished the 1978–1979 season 24–5. Forward David Greenwood earned all-American honors for the second year in a row.

Cunningham stepped down as head coach after his second season. He finished his coaching career with an overall record of 50–8. Cunningham achieved the highest winning percentage (.862) of any coach in UCLA basketball history.

UCLA HIRES LARRY BROWN

Former Denver Nuggets coach Larry Brown led the Bruins for the next two years. Brown inherited a team that wasn't listed

UCLA forward Kiki Vandeweghe (#55) goes to the hole during the 1980 NCAA championship game against Louisville. The Bruins led late in the game but lost the title match 59–54.

in the top twenty at the start of the 1979–1980 season. But his underranked players made it to the national championship game that year. The Bruins crushed Idaho State 82–40 in the season opener. The team finished 22–10 and earned a bid to the NCAA tournament.

UCLA upset Purdue 67–62 in the Final Four. On March 24, 1980, the Bruins faced Louisville for the national championship. This marked the first time since Wooden retired that UCLA advanced to the title game.

The Bruins led by four with 4:32 left on the clock. Forward Ernest Maurice "Kiki" Vandeweghe, a two-time academic all-American, missed a layup that would have given UCLA a six-point lead. Louisville then went on a 9–0 run and captured the title crown 59–54. The Bruins wouldn't get a shot at the national title for another fifteen years.

UCLA posted a 21–6 record the following season. The Bruins returned to the NCAA tournament but were destroyed by Brigham Young 78–55 in the second round. Brown left UCLA after the 1981 season. He had a 42–17 overall record after two seasons.

LARRY FARMER TAKES OVER

Another UCLA basketball star took over the Bruins at the start of the 1981–1982 season. Larry Farmer, who played for John Wooden in the 1970s, coached the Bruins for three years.

UCLA posted a 21–6 record during Farmer's first season at the helm. The Bruins improved to 23–6 the next year. The team won the Pacific-10 Conference and advanced to the NCAA tournament that season. The Bruins fell in the second round to Utah, 67–61. Forward Kenny Fields and guard Rod Foster made the all-Conference team during that 1982–1983 season.

The Bruins dropped to 17–10 during Farmer's third and final year. The team finished fourth in the Pacific-10 Conference and did not earn a bid to the NCAA tournament. Farmer resigned after the 1984 season. He left with a 61–23 overall record.

UCLA PICKS ALL-AMERICAN WALT HAZZARD

The Bruins named two-time all-American Walt Hazzard as the team's next head coach. The team finished 23–6 during Hazzard's first year. UCLA won the Pacific-10 championship that season. It also made its first appearance in the National

ALL-TIME LEADER IN NBA PICKS

The National Basketball Association (NBA) has drafted more players from UCLA than from any other college in the country. Records show the NBA picked 108 Bruins in drafts held between 1948 and 2011. The NBA selected 33 UCLA players in the first rounds of drafts held during that time period. And three of its players were the number one draft picks in the country. These players were:

- **Guard Walt Hazzard.** The Los Angeles Lakers drafted the two-time all-American in 1964. He played in the NBA for ten years.
- **Center Lew Alcindor (Kareem Abdul-Jabbar).** Milwaukee drafted the three-time all-American in 1969. He played for the Bucks and the Los Angeles Lakers during his twenty years in the NBA.
- **Center Bill Walton.** Portland selected this all-American in 1974. He later played for the San Diego Clippers and Boston Celtics during his thirteen years in the NBA.

Other UCLA stars drafted by the NBA in first rounds include guard Gail Goodrich (1965); forward Sydney Wickes (1971); forward Marque Johnson (1977); forward Kiki Vandeweghe (1980); forward Reggie Miller (1987); guard Pooh Richardson (1989); guard Tyus Edney (1995); guard Aaron Affalo (2007); forward/center Jerome Moiso (2000); center Kevin Love (2008); and guard Jrue Holiday (2009). The NBA also drafted two brothers who played for UCLA. New Jersey picked forward Ed O'Bannon in 1995. In 1997 Detroit drafted his younger brother, forward Charles O'Bannon.

Invitational Tournament (NIT). That is a second-level post-season tournament.

The Bruins squeaked past Indiana 65–62 to win the NIT. Guard Reggie Miller drained 18 points in the championship game. He was named the tournament's Most Valuable Player.

UCLA posted a disappointing 15–14 record during Hazzard's second year. But it returned to the winner's circle a year later. The Bruins finished the 1986–1987 season 25–7. The team came in first in the Pacific-10 and won the conference tournament.

In the first round of the NCAA tournament, UCLA steamrolled Central Michigan 92–73. The Bruins lost in the next round to Wyoming, 78–68. UCLA's Reggie Miller posted the tournament's highest scoring average with 28 points per game.

UCLA trampled Oral Roberts 119–79 in the opening game of its 1987–1988 season. But the season went downhill from there. The Bruins ended the year 16–14 and did not earn a bid to the NCAA tournament. Hazzard left UCLA in 1988 with an overall record of 77–47.

UCLA CHASES ELEVENTH NCAA TITLE

The Bruins regained their rule of the hardwood under UCLA's next head coach, Jim Harrick. He made his coaching debut on November 26, 1988. The Bruins crushed Texas Tech 84–62 in the season opener. UCLA finished the year 21–10. The Bruins lost to North Carolina 88–81 in the second round of the NCAA tournament.

UCLA returned to the national tournament every year during Harrick's tenure. But it advanced only once past the Elite Eight—in 1995. All-American forward Ed O'Bannon led the Bruins to a record 32–1 season that year. And UCLA earned another shot at the title crown.

BUZZER-BEATER SECOND-ROUND WIN

The Bruins played one of the most unforgettable games in NCAA history during the second round of the 1995 tournament. UCLA faced the Missouri Tigers. The Bruins were down by eight at the half. They closed the gap to one point with 4.8 seconds on the clock.

UCLA put the ball—and its future—in the hands of Tyus Edney. The senior point guard raced down the court. He dodged one defender with a behind-the-back dribble. Edney then drove over the outstretched hands of 6-foot-9 (206 cm) Derek Grimm. He sank a layup at the buzzer. The Bruins won, 75–74, to advance in the tournament. "This is the biggest shot of my life," Edney told reporters after the game.

UCLA sailed through the next three rounds. The Bruins faced Arkansas, the defending national champion, in the title match. Edney left the game early because of a wrist injury. Forward Ed O'Bannon and guard Toby Bailey picked up the slack. O'Bannon scored 30 points and Bailey added 26. The Bruins captured the 1995 championship title 89–78. The victory gave UCLA its first NCAA crown in twenty years.

But UCLA didn't stay on top for long. The Bruins lost to Princeton 43–41 in the first round of the 1996 NCAA tournament. Scandal rocked UCLA's basketball program a few

UCLA coach Jim Harrick congratulates forward Ed O'Bannon (#31) after the Bruins defeat Arkansas 89–78 to win the 1995 NCAA championship. O'Bannon scored 30 points in that title game.

months later. The university discovered that Harrick lied about a recruiting violation. UCLA fired the head coach two weeks before the start of the 1996–1997 season.

The university then made another shocking move. Bruins fans couldn't believe the young coach UCLA named to replace Harrick.

CHAPTER 4

THE BRUINS IN THE TWENTY-FIRST CENTURY

ension swirled through UCLA's Pauley Pavilion. The opening game of the Bruins' 1996–1997 season was on the line. UCLA faced a scrappy Tulsa team, which forced the battle into overtime. Two seconds remained on the clock. The score was tied 76–76. Tulsa's Zac Bennet stepped up to the free-throw line. He missed his first shot but nailed the second. Tulsa upset UCLA 77–76 in that November 20, 1996, preseason NIT tournament game.

A stunned Steve Lavin stood on the Bruins sideline. His first win—in his debut as UCLA's eleventh head coach—just slipped away. The thirty-two-year-old Lavin replaced longtime coach Jim Harrick, who was fired two weeks before the season started. UCLA's decision to hire Lavin as interim coach shocked many fans. Lavin was too young, they said. And he had no experience as a head coach. He'd served as Harrick's assistant for two years.

But Lavin and the Bruins shook off that opening game defeat. The team fought its way to 13–7 by February. UCLA also regained the pride it lost during a crushing 109–61 defeat to Stanford in January. The 48-point loss marked the worst blowout in UCLA history.

The Bruins wanted revenge. They found it when the two rivals met again on February 8, 1997. Forward Charles O'Bannon ignited his team. He scored 23 points and grabbed 12 rebounds. The Bruins pounded Stanford 87–68.

LAVIN LEADS BRUINS TO ELITE EIGHT

Three days later, UCLA removed the "interim" label from Lavin's title. He signed a four-year contract reportedly worth $500,000 a year—much more than the $16,000 Lavin had earned as an assistant.

The Bruins finished 24–8 during Lavin's first season. UCLA clinched first place in the Pacific-10 Conference and advanced to the NCAA tournament. But the team stumbled and lost 80–72 to Minnesota in the Elite Eight.

UCLA returned to the NCAA tournament the following season. The team struggled in the first two rounds. It faced number two Kentucky in the Sweet 16. The Wildcats trounced the Bruins 94–68 and later won the 1998 national title. UCLA ended the year 24–9.

UCLA center Jelani McCoy drives for two in the opening game of the Bruins' 1996–1997 season. The Bruins lost a heartbreaker to Tulsa 77–76 in the final seconds of the game.

An animated Steve Lavin tries to get his players' attention during their January 18, 2001, game against Arizona State. Lavin coached UCLA for seven seasons.

The Bruins lost a heartbreaker to Detroit 53–56 in the first round of the 1999 NCAA tournament. UCLA finished that year 22–9.

REPEAT TRIPS TO THE SWEET 16

Lavin and his team entered the 1999–2000 season ranked thirteenth in the nation. UCLA crushed its first three opponents. In game three, the Bruins destroyed Morgan State 100–39. The team capped its 21–12 season by winning eight of its last nine games.

UCLA TRIVIA

How much do you know about UCLA and its basketball program? Here are some trivia questions to test your knowledge:

- *Who are the only two brothers to be named all-American at UCLA?* Charles and Ed O'Bannon. Ed, a forward, was named an all-American in 1995. Charles, also a forward, received that honor in 1997.
- *What was the largest crowd in Pauley Pavilion history?* A record 13,478 fans packed the arena on February 23, 1997, for the UCLA-Duke game.
- *Who were the first UCLA players to have their numbers retired?* On February 3, 1990, UCLA retired the numbers of Lew Alcindor (#33), Bill Walton (#32), Ann Meyers-Drysdale (#15), and Denise Curry (#12).
- *Which three NCAA coaches have won thirty games in three consecutive years?* The three coaches are Ben Howland of UCLA (2006–2008), Adolph Rupp of Kentucky (1947–1949), and John Calipari of Memphis (2006–2008).

The Bruins breezed through the early rounds of the NCAA tournament. But UCLA buckled under pressure from Iowa State in the Sweet 16. The Bruins lost 80–56.

UCLA fought its way back to the Sweet 16 the next two years. During the 2001 NCAA tournament, the Bruins cruised past Hofstra (61–48) and Utah State (75–50) in the early rounds. But UCLA lost again in the Sweet 16—this time to Duke (63–76). The Bruins ended the year 23–9.

In 2002, UCLA returned to the Sweet 16 for the third year in a row. The Bruins coasted past Mississippi, 80–58, in the opening round. The team eked out a 105–101 double-overtime win against Cincinnati in round two. UCLA faced Missouri in the Sweet 16. The Bruins lost 73–82 and ended the year 21–12.

UCLA FIRES LAVIN

The 2002–2003 season turned into a nightmare for Lavin and his team. UCLA recorded its first losing season since 1948. The Bruins ended the year 10–19. Three days after the Bruins' final game—a 74–75 loss to Oregon—UCLA fired Lavin.

The Associated Press wasn't surprised by the move. "It was a stunningly poor year for a program that has won a record eleven national championships: ten under John Wooden in the 1960s and 1970s, and one under Jim Harrick in 1995—when Lavin was an assistant coach," the wire service wrote in a March 17, 2003, story.

Lavin compiled a 145–78 record during seven seasons. He recruited future NBA stars to UCLA, including Trevor Ariza, Cedric Bozeman, Baron Davis, and Jason Kapono. Forward Charles O'Bannon also became an all-American during Lavin's tenure.

HOWLAND NAMED UCLA'S TWELFTH HEAD COACH

UCLA hired Ben Howland—the man who turned around the University of Pittsburgh's ailing basketball program—as its next head coach. Howland took over in April 2003. The Southern California native called the position with the Bruins his "dream job," according to United Press International.

Howland's first year at UCLA wasn't too dreamy, though. The Bruins barely squeaked out a 68–67 win over Vermont in

Howland's debut as head coach. Later in the season, the team took a nosedive. UCLA finished 11–17 and posted its first back-to-back losing seasons since the 1940s.

The 2004–2005 season seemed to signal the return of UCLA's power on the hardwood. The Bruins started with a four-game winning streak. Three freshmen guards fueled the team's success: Arron Afflalo, Jordan Farmar, and Josh Shipp. UCLA returned to the NCAA tournament. But the team fell in the first round to Texas Tech 66–78. The Bruins finished the year 18–11.

UCLA upped its game the following season, 2005–2006. The Bruins flexed their basketball muscles and advanced to the NCAA's championship game. This marked the first time in eleven years that UCLA battled for the national crown.

The Bruins sailed through the tournament's first five rounds. The championship game pitted UCLA against Florida. UCLA struggled and lost the 2006 title match 57–73. The Bruins ended the year 32–7.

FINAL FOUR APPEARANCES

The mighty Bruins didn't let their guard down the following year. The team battled its way back to the Final Four in 2007. UCLA overpowered Indiana (54–49), Pittsburgh (64–55), and Kansas (68–55) in the tournament's early rounds. The Bruins faced Florida again—this time in the semifinals. UCLA lost the rematch 66–76. It ended the season 30–6.

The Bruins returned for another Final Four showdown in 2008. UCLA squashed Mississippi Valley 79–29 in the NCAA tournament's opening round. Freshman guard Kevin Love supplied the firepower the Bruins needed to win the next three rounds. But UCLA's Final Four journey ended with a 63–78 defeat to Memphis.

UCLA basketball fans cheer as their team crushes the tenth-ranked Arizona Wildcats 71–49 on February 29, 2011. The blowout marked UCLA's last home game before the university renovated Pauley Pavilion.

Howland couldn't hide his disappointment. "It's hard to be here three years in a row and not come away with a championship," he told reporters after the game. The Bruins finished the 2007–2008 season 35–4.

UCLA's record slipped to 26–9 the following year. The Bruins also suffered a 20-point loss to Villanova (69–89) in the second round of the NCAA tournament. Howland's record plunged deeper during his seventh year on the bench. UCLA finished the 2009–2010 season with a 14–18 record. Was UCLA's basketball dynasty on the verge of collapse? Could the Bruins claw their way back to the top?

UCLA unleashed two six-game winning streaks during the 2010–2011 season. The Bruins finished 23–11 and returned to the NCAA tournament. But Florida—for the third time since 2006—crushed UCLA's dream to win another national championship. The Bruins crumbled 73–65 in the Sweet 16.

CONTROVERSY ENGULFS UCLA

Controversy surrounded the Bruins during the 2011–2012 season. A March 2012 investigation by *Sports Illustrated* exposed problems with Howland's recent teams. "Fistfights broke out among teammates," the story said. "Several players routinely used alcohol and drugs, sometimes before practice. One player intentionally injured teammates but received no punishment." The story pointed to UCLA forward Reeves Nelson as a key figure in a number of the incidents. Howland dismissed Nelson from the team in December 2011 for "continued conduct issues."

Howland said he had made mistakes and promised to fix the problems. UCLA stood by its coach. The Bruins finished the 2011-2012 season with a 19-14 record. The team didn't play in the 2012 NCAA tournament.

UCLA improved to 25-10 in the 2012–2013 season and captured the Pac-12 conference title. The Bruins advanced to the NCAA tournament, but suffered a crushing 83-63 loss to Minnesota in the opening round. Two days later, UCLA fired Howland. He finished his ten-year career at UCLA with a 233-107 record.

Although the Bruins have struggled in recent years, former head coach Gary Cunningham isn't worried about UCLA's future on the hardwood – or its legacy as one the most winning teams in college basketball. "All oars are (going) in the right direction," he told Rosen Publishing.

1891: John Naismith invents the game of basketball.

1919: Fred Cozens coaches UCLA's first men's basketball team.

1928: Forward Jack Ketchum becomes UCLA's first basketball player to earn all-Conference honors.

1931: Forward Dick Linthicum becomes UCLA's first all-American.

1939: Baseball legend Jackie Robinson makes his debut on UCLA's basketball team.

1948: John Wooden takes over as UCLA's fourth head basketball coach.

1962: UCLA advances to the Final Four for the first time.

1964: UCLA captures its first NCAA national title in a 98–83 victory over Duke.

1974: UCLA's eighty-eight-game winning streak ends in a 71–70 loss to Notre Dame.

1975: UCLA captures its tenth NCAA title under coach John Wooden with a 92–85 win over Kentucky. Wooden retires from the game.

1995: UCLA captures its eleventh NCAA title with an 89–78 win over Arkansas.

2008: UCLA wins a record 35 games in the season.

2010: Legendary coach John Wooden dies at age 99.

2013: UCLA's lineup includes three star freshmen: Jordan Adams, Kyle Anderson, and Shabazz Muhammad. By early March, the Bruins had a 22–7 record and shared the Pac-12 lead with Oregon.

GLOSSARY

dynasty A group, family, or team that is powerful or successful for a long period of time.

Final Four The last four teams remaining from the sixty-four college teams that compete in the annual NCAA Tournament.

inaugural The first in a series of similar events.

interim Appointed to serve temporarily.

layup A one-handed banked shot made from near the basket.

legacy Something handed down from one generation to the next.

milestone A significant event or point in development.

playmaker A player who scores many points or creates opportunities for players to score.

prestigious Recognized for success or importance; honored.

rebound The act of gaining possession of the basketball following a missed shot that bounces off the backboard or basket rim.

scandal A situation or event that causes public outrage, anger, or embarrassment.

showdown A decisive test or contest.

steamroll To overpower or crush.

taunt To tease or ridicule.

titan A person or thing of great power or importance.

underdog A competitor that is expected to lose a contest.

Canada Basketball

1 Westside Drive, Suite 11
Etobicoke, ON M9C 1B2
Canada
(416) 614-8037
Web site: http://www.basketball.ca

Canada Basketball is the national sporting organization and governing body for amateur basketball in Canada. It is recognized as such by the International Amateur Basketball Federation (FIBA) and the government of Canada.

Naismith Memorial Basketball Hall of Fame

1000 Hall of Fame Avenue
Springfield, MA 01105
(413) 781-6500
Web site: http://www.hoophall.com

The Naismith Memorial Basketball Hall of Fame honors the best basketball players, coaches, referees, and other contributors to the game. Its educational department provides stories, activities, and inspirational messages for young fans.

National Association of Intercollegiate Athletics (NAIA)

1200 Grand Boulevard
Kansas City, MO 64106
(816) 595-8000
Web site: http://www.naia.org

The National Association of Intercollegiate Athletics is the governing body for athletics programs at nearly three hundred colleges and universities in the United States and Canada.

National Collegiate Athletic Association (NCAA)

700 W. Washington Street

P.O. Box 6222

Indianapolis, IN 46206-6222

(317) 917-6222

Web site: http://www.ncaa.org

The National Collegiate Athletic Association (NCAA) is a nonprofit organization that serves student-athletes. It organizes the athletic programs at more than one thousand colleges and universities in the United States and Canada.

United States Olympic Committee

27 South Tejon

Colorado Springs, CO 80903

(719) 632-5551

Web site: http://www.teamusa.org

The United States Olympic Committee is responsible for training and funding U.S. teams for the Olympics, Paralympics, Youth Olympics, Pan American, and Parapan American Games.

WEB SITES

Due to the changing nature of Internet links, Rosen Publishing has developed an online list of Web sites related to the subject of this book. This site is updated regularly. Please use this link to access the list:

http://www.rosenlinks.com/AMWT/UCLABB

FOR FURTHER READING

ESPN. *ESPN College Basketball Encyclopedia: The Complete History of the Men's Game.* New York, NY: Ballantine Books/ESPN Books, 2009.

Hoffer, Richard, John Wooden, Dick Enberg, and Denny Crum. *Wooden: Basketball & Beyond: The Official UCLA Retrospective.* San Diego, CA: Skybox Press, 2011.

Kelly, Greg. *The College Basketball Book.* New York, NY: Sports Illustrated, 2011.

LeBoutillier, Nate. *The Best of Everything Basketball Book* (All-Time Best of Sports). Mankato, MN: Capstone Press, 2011.

Schaller, Bob, and Dave Harnish. *The Everything Kids' Basketball Book: The All-Time Greats, Legendary Teams, Today's Superstars—and Tips on Playing Like a Pro.* Avon, MA: Adams Media, 2009.

Schulte, Mary E. *The Final Four: All About College Basketball's Biggest Event* (Winner Takes All). Mankato, MN: Capstone Press, 2012.

Silverman, Drew. *UCLA Bruins* (Inside College Basketball). Minneapolis, MN: ABDO Publishing Co., 2012.

Smith, John Matthew. *The Sons of Westwood: John Wooden, UCLA, and the Dynasty That Changed College Basketball.* Urbana, IL: University of Illinois Press, 2013.

Wiseman, Blaine, and Aaron Carr. *Basketball* (The Greatest Players). New York, NY: AV2 by Weigl, 2012.

Wooden, John, and Steve Jamison. *The Wisdom of Wooden: My Century On and Off the Court.* New York, NY: McGraw Hill, 2010.

BIBLIOGRAPHY

Associated Press. "College Basketball—Men—Lavin Fired After UCLA's First Losing Season Since 1948." SI.com, March 18, 2003. Retrieved October 30, 2012 (http://sportsillustrated.cnn .com/basketball/college/news/2003/03/17/lavin_fired_ap).

Associated Press. "Lavin Gets the Gig: Interim Status Is Replaced by 4-Year Vote of Confidence." *Los Angeles Times*, February 12, 1997. Retrieved October 30, 2012 (http://articles.latimes .com/1997-02-12/sports/sp-27840_1_steve-lavin).

"Bruin Five Opens Season Tonight." *Long Beach Press-Telegram*, December 3, 1948.

CBS Sports. "NCAA Tournament History." CBSSports.com. Retrieved October 30, 2012 (http://www.cbssports.com/college basketball/ncaa-tournament/history/yearbyyear/index).

Cunningham, Gary. Interview with the author. August 7, 2012.

Dohrmann, George. "Special Report: Not the UCLA Way." *Sports Illustrated*, March 5, 2012. Retrieved October 30, 2012 (http: //sportsillustrated.cnn.com/2012/magazine/02/28/ucla/ index.html).

Fleder, Rob. *The Basketball Book*. New York, NY: Time Books, 2007.

Hammel, Bob. "At Last! IU and UCLA Collide." Hoosier Historia, November 28, 1975. Retrieved October 30, 2012 (http://www .heraldtimesonline.com/hoosiershq/historia/1976/?sid=43).

Howard-Cooper, Scott. *The Bruin 100: The Greatest Games in the History of UCLA Basketball*. Lenexa, KS: Addax Publishing Group, 1999.

Krider, Dave. "John Wooden: An American Beauty (1910–2010)." MaxPreps.com. Retrieved October 30, 2012 (http://www

.maxpreps.com/news/GIVf_XCkED-lugAcxJTdpg/john-wooden--an-american-beauty-(1910-2010).htm

Luther, Claudia. "Coach John Wooden, 1910–2010." UCLA Newsroom, June 4, 2010. Retrieved October 30, 2012 (http://newsroom.ucla.edu/portal/ucla/john-wooden-dies-84109.aspx).

Medley, H. Anthony. *UCLA Basketball: The Real Story*. Los Angeles, CA: Galant Press, 1972.

Rippey, Tom P., Paul F. Wilson, and Al Netzer. *Bruinology Trivia Challenge: UCLA Bruins Basketball*. 2nd ed. Lewis Center, OH: Kick the Ball Ltd., 2008.

UCLA Official Athletic Site. "John Wooden: A Coaching Legend, October 14, 1910–June 4, 2010." UCLABruins.com. Retrieved October 30, 2012 (http://www.uclabruins.com/sports/m-baskbl/spec-rel/ucla-wooden-page.html).

UCLA Official Athletic Site. "UCLA 2006–2007 Men's Basketball Media Guide." UCLABruins.com. Retrieved October 30, 2012 (http://grfx.cstv.com/photos/schools/ucla/sports/m-baskbl/auto_pdf/MBBGuide99-128.pdf).

Washburn, Jon. "What If a Snow Storm Hadn't Kept John Wooden from Going to Minnesota?" Midwest Sports Fans, March 27, 2012. Retrieved October 30, 2012 (http://www.midwestsportsfans.com/2012/03/what-if-a-snow-storm-hadnt-kept-john-wooden-from-going-to-minnesota).

Wolff, Alex. "Something Special About the First: How '64 Bruins Made John Wooden." SI.com, June 4, 2010. Retrieved October 30, 2012 (http://sportsillustrated.cnn.com/2010/writers/alexander_wolff/06/03/wooden.1964/index.html).

Yoon, Peter. "UCLA Dismisses Reeves Nelson." ESPNLosAngeles.com, December 9, 2011. Retrieved October 30, 2012 (http://espn.go.com/los-angeles/ncb/story/_/id/7336148/ucla-bruins-dismiss-reeves-nelson-team).

INDEX

ABOUT THE AUTHOR

Lisa Wade McCormick is an award-winning writer and investigative reporter. She has also written sixteen nonfiction books for children. Lisa and her family live in Kansas City, Missouri. She often visits schools and libraries with her golden retriever, who is a Reading Education Assistance Dog (READ). The mission of the READ program is to improve children's literacy skills by giving struggling readers the opportunity to read to dogs.

PHOTO CREDITS